Joel, Jesper, and Julia

Joel, Jesper, and Julia

by Åke Eriksson

Carolrhoda Books, Inc./Minneapolis

LIBRARY OF CONGRESS CATALOGING-IN-PUBLICATION DATA

Eriksson, Åke, 1924-
   [Joel, Jesper, och Julia. English]
   Joel, Jesper, and Julia / by Åke Eriksson.
      p.   cm.
   Translation of: Joel, Jesper, och Julia.
   Summary: Living on a farm, Joel cares for a little piglet and
tries to save the animal when Dad says it's time for slaughter.
   ISBN 0-87614-419-9:
   [1. Pigs—Fiction. 2. Farm life—Fiction.] I. Title.
PZ7.E72587Jo   1990
[E]—dc20-   89-25116
                                                       CIP
                                                        AC

Manufactured in the United States of America

1 2 3 4 5 6 7 8 9 10 00 99 98 97 96 95 94 93 92 91 90

Joel lives on a farm, way out in the country.
On any sunny day, you can see Joel playing
with his best friend, Jesper the cat.
Jesper is an expert at all the games —
hide-and-seek, catch, and tag.

One day last spring, while Joel and Jesper were playing tag,
they ran into the barn. From over in the corner,
they heard a clamor of grunts and squeals.
The big mama pig had had piglets—thirteen of them!

But thirteen is a bad number for piglets.
A mama pig can only feed twelve pigs at a time,
so one poor little piglet had to go without.
The leftover pig was born last and was smaller than all the rest.

While Joel and Jesper were watching the little pig,
Joel's father came into the barn shaking his head.
"It's too bad," he said, "but we'll have to do away with
the little one. She won't be able to take care of herself."

"Oh, Dad, we can't do that!" Joel cried. Jesper meowed in agreement.

"She'll only get sick and die," his father explained.

"No, she won't," said Joel, "because I'll take care of her."

"Well, I don't know," his father said.
"You don't look big enough to take care of a pig."

"I am too," said Joel, and he picked up the little pig.
"I'll show you."

So that very morning, and every morning afterward, Joel and Jesper went to the barn to take some milk from the big mama pig.

She was always rather nasty, so Joel had to be very careful. All the little piglets were nasty too. They squealed at Joel to leave some milk for them.

Joel mixed the pig's milk with some cow's milk for his hungry
little piglet. She drank in quick gulps, making funny grunting sounds.

Joel and Jesper decided to call her Julia.

Julia was a fabulous eater.
Jesper watched as she got bigger

and bigger

and bigger.

Soon Jesper had taught Julia how to play
pounce, hide-and-seek, and tag.

But teaching her to climb a tree was another story entirely.

Joel, Jesper, and Julia became the best of friends.
Wherever Joel and Jesper went, Julia was right behind . . .

. . . especially when they went to the bakery.
Nothing tasted better than those
gooey caramel rolls.

One day Joel put Julia and Jesper into the pigpen.
"Okay, you two," he said, "now you be good.
I'm going to a wedding with Mom and Dad."

That afternoon, inside the little country church,
the wedding march began to play.
All the people stood up to watch the bride.
But who did they see instead?
Julia and Jesper, of course, grinning from ear to ear.

Julia and Jesper were feeling quite smart.
They had managed to sneak out of the pen
and find their way to the church, all by themselves!

Joel's parents were not pleased.
"Take them home this instant," his father scolded.

So Joel led them out of the church.
They all felt pretty bad as they walked home . . .

. . . until Julia decided that the day was made for napping, and that there's nothing better than a rest in the sun.

So Joel and Jesper stretched themselves out beside her, and once again, the world was grand.

Summer passed into autumn, and autumn into winter.

As white flakes fell like goose feathers from the sky,
Julia squealed with delight. It was her first snow.

That day Joel and his father had a serious talk. "Son," said Joel's father,
"Christmastime is coming, and all the pigs are fat and ready.
The truck from the slaughterhouse is coming this afternoon."

"But, Dad," Joel protested.

"I know it's hard," his father replied,
"but it has to be done. Julia has had a nice time
all spring, summer, and fall.
And this is what she was raised for."

As soon as his father left, Joel ran to the back of the house and led Julia up the stairs. "Shhh" he whispered, so Julia tried her best to tiptoe. Once they were in his room, Joel put Julia in his closet. It was a tight fit.

Just as Joel managed to squeeze the door shut . . .

. . . his father walked in the room. "The pigs are ready," his father announced, "all except Julia. Have you seen her?"

"Oink" the closet grunted, and Joel and Jesper started to cough.

"Have you caught a cold?" asked Joel's father, trying to look stern. "Your cough sounds an awful lot like a pig in the closet. But you couldn't possibly have a pig in your closet, could you?"

"A pig in the closet?" Joel mumbled.

Fortunately, the slaughterhouse truck left—without Julia.
Joel and Jesper sighed in relief. Then they made their plans.
That night, when it was dark, Joel, Jesper, and Julia
slipped away into the woods.

They wandered silently through the trees, listening to the night owls.
Julia sniffed the ground, looking for a place to stay.
Then she found it—the perfect place for a den—
a soft mossy spot under a big old fir tree.

For the rest of the winter, Joel and Jesper came to visit Julia as often
as they could. They brought her scraps of food and,
once in a while, even a sweet, gooey roll.

At home Joel's mother watched her son proudly. "I know you're sad that Julia disappeared," she said to him, "but you've been very brave about it." Joel smiled, and Jesper began to purr.

Joel's father looked at the two of them. "Hmmm," he said, "I just wonder where Julia went." Joel and Jesper didn't say anything.

One day, when Joel and Jesper were out in the woods,
they discovered that Julia was not alone.
Next to her, peering out from her den, was a handsome wild boar.
He'd moved in with her!

Joel and Jesper decided to call him Julius.

At last winter came to an end, and once again it was spring.

Joel and Jesper spent their days frolicking in the fresh sunny air.
But they missed Julia.

One morning they ran through the fields and into the woods
to pay their friend a visit. As they peeked around the corner,
what did they see but thirteen little piglets!

Striped and grunting, the piglets were all pushing
to get close to Julia. But one little pig stood by himself.

He was the thirteenth piglet, and there was no room left for him!

That afternoon Joel's parents got a surprise too. Joel and Jesper came walking out of the woods with a little pig that looked just like a wild boar! Before his parents could say anything, Joel said firmly, "This is Jonathan, and I'm going to take care of him."

And that was the end of that.